# zenda

## Lost on Aquaria

Dedicated
in the memory of
Rosie

# zenda

## Lost on Aquaria

created by
Ken Petti and John Amodeo

written with
Cassandra Westwood

Grosset & Dunlap ∾ New York

Copyright © 2004 by Ken Petti & John Amodeo. ZENDA is a trademark of Ken Petti & John Amodeo. All rights reserved. Published by Grosset & Dunlap, a division of Penguin Young Readers Group,
345 Hudson Street, New York, New York 10014.
GROSSET & DUNLAP is a trademark of
Penguin Group (USA) Inc. Printed in the U.S.A.

Library of Congress Cataloging-in-Publication Data

Petti, Ken.
Lost on Aquaria / created by Ken Petti and John Amodeo ;
written with Cassandra Westwood.
p. cm. — (Zenda ; 4)
Summary: While on a school trip to Aquaria, one of Azureblue's moons, Zenda is separated from the group with her nemesis, Alexandra, and they must work together to reach safety while avoiding the monster born of their own doubt and fear.
ISBN 0-448-43256-0 (pbk.)
[1. Survival—Fiction. 2. Fear—Fiction. 3. School field trips—Fiction. 4. Fantasy.]
I. Amodeo, John, 1949 May 19- II. Westwood, Cassandra. III. Title. IV. Series.
PZ7.P448125Lo 2004
[Fic]—dc22
2004001432

ISBN 0-448-43256-0        10  9  8  7  6  5  4  3  2  1

# Contents

So many things have happened to me since I turned twelve-and-a-half!

First, I got into big trouble when I decided to sneak a peek at my gazing ball. Every boy and girl on Azureblue gets one before he or she turns thirteen. Over time, the gazing ball reveals musings that help you on life's path.

That's what usually happens, anyway. Instead, I broke my gazing ball. Now I have to wait until the missing pieces appear to me, one at a time, to get my musings. I've recovered five pieces so far.

It wasn't easy. So far, I've stolen a dangerous plant, got transported to another dimension, and traveled all the way to the planet Crystallin, where I faced a poisonous snake. I thought things couldn't get much stranger. But I was wrong.

I just got back from Aquaria, one of the four moons that orbit Azureblue. Aquaria is a wild place, filled with waterfalls, raging rivers, and unusual plants and animals. I went there for a school trip— and ended up getting lost! All because of Alexandra White. That girl makes me so angry sometimes!

You'll see what I mean. And if you ever go to Aquaria, be careful! You don't want to get lost there—trust me.

Cosmically yours,
Zenda

*Worries*

*Zenda's bare feet crunched against fallen leaves on the forest floor as she darted around the trees. She had to get away.*

*It was coming after her. Zenda could feel its presence behind her, getting faster and faster with each step.*

*She wanted to look behind her, to see how close it was, but she was too afraid of what she might see.*

*And then the forest suddenly ended, and she found herself at the edge of a cliff. There was nothing but blue sky and fluffy clouds in front of her.*

*Zenda skidded to a stop. There was nowhere to run. It was even closer now. She had to turn around. Had to face it. She slowly turned her head.*

"Aaaaaaaaaaah!" Zenda screamed and sat up in bed, her heart pounding.

It was just a dream. The same dream she had had for three nights in a row.

The door to Zenda's room creaked open. Her mother, Verbena, stepped inside.

Moonlight shone through the window and lit up Verbena's worried face.

"Are you all right?" she asked. Without waiting for an answer, she came and sat on the edge of Zenda's bed.

"Just a nightmare," Zenda said. "I've had it before." She leaned back against the mountain of pillows piled at the head of her bed. Seeing her mother's soft, honey-colored eyes made her instantly feel calmer.

Verbena brushed a strand of reddish-gold hair away from Zenda's face. "Sometimes we work out our worries and fears through our dreams," she said. "Is there something you're worried about?"

Zenda felt a twinge in her stomach. She *was* worried about something. But whenever she tried to talk about it, she couldn't find the words. Zenda just nodded.

Verbena seemed to understand. She leaned over and kissed Zenda on the forehead.

"Let me know if you want to talk," she said. "In the meantime, try some Relaxation elixir. You need to get a good sleep tonight."

Verbena quietly left the room and closed the door behind her. Zenda sat up in bed. The elixir wasn't a bad idea. She tiptoed across the floor to her dresser. Bottles of lotions, potions, and elixirs made by her family's karmaceutical company crowded its surface. Zenda squinted in the moonlight until she found the Relaxation elixir. She dabbed some on her temples and wrists, inhaling the scent of lavender and basil.

Zenda climbed back under the covers. Oscar, her little brown dog, snuggled up beside her. Zenda had to smile. Nothing—not even Zenda's scream—would wake Oscar from a sound sleep.

She closed her eyes and took a deep breath. Her mother was right—she did need her rest. Tomorrow, all of the seventh-year students from the Cobalt School for Girls and the Cobalt School for Boys were taking a two-day trip to Aquaria, one of Azureblue's four moons.

Marion Rose, Zenda's teacher, had called it a survival trip. Aquaria was an unsettled nature preserve. The students would be camping out, foraging for their own food, building their own shelter, and making their own heat.

The very idea of the survival trip was one of the things that worried Zenda. She loved being outdoors, but surviving in the wild was another story. She liked her comfy bed and her father Vetiver's delicious, wholesome cooking.

"Don't worry if you don't know how to do any of these things," Marion Rose had said. "The only skill you need on this trip is an ability to cooperate!"

That hadn't made Zenda feel much better. Because the other thing that worried her was the idea of going so far away, surrounded by all of her classmates.

The seventh year of school had not been an easy one for Zenda. During this year, every boy and girl on Azureblue received a gazing ball. As he or she studied the ball, it would reveal thirteen musings—words of advice to help with the transition to adulthood. But Zenda had accidentally broken her ball, so instead of going to gazing ball class with all of her friends, she had been left on her own to recover the missing pieces. She had five so far, but still had a long way to go before she could join the others again.

Before her gazing ball broke, Zenda had already felt a separation between her and most of the girls in school. It started when Zenda had showed signs of *kani*—the ability to communicate with plants. Each person on Azureblue was born with a special gift, but it almost never made an appearance until one's thirteenth birthday—after gazing ball training was complete. Zenda's early gift had set her apart from other children.

Some people, she knew, were suspicious of it, maybe even a little jealous. Zenda could never understand that. Her *kani* never worked properly, and usually got her into embarrassing situations. Besides, she wasn't even sure she wanted the gift of *kani*, anyway.

And now Zenda was going to spend a weekend far away on Aquaria, stuck with a bunch of people who thought she was weird. She sighed and picked up a colorful doll lying on the pillow beside her.

"How am I going to make it through the weekend, Luna?" Zenda asked.

Luna smiled back at Zenda with her stitched-on mouth. The doll had belonged to Zenda's grandmother, Delphina, when she was just a little girl. Delphina had passed it on to Zenda before she died. Whenever Zenda talked to Luna, it felt like her grandmother was near.

Zenda sighed. She usually took Luna

everywhere with her. But she knew the other students would think she was babyish if she took a doll with her on the trip. Luna would just have to stay at home.

As Zenda stared at Luna, she saw her grandmother's face in her mind's eye: her smiling blue eyes and soft, white hair. A memory came back to Zenda at the same time.

It was summertime, and Delphina had taken Zenda berry picking with Mykal and Camille. She and her friends were probably only about eight years old. They had eaten more berries that day than they had put in Delphina's wicker basket.

As they walked home, Delphina had said something to Zenda that she had never forgotten.

"Good friends are sweeter than ripe berries, Zenda," she had said, nodding toward Mykal and Camille. "As long as you have friends, you will never be alone in life."

Zenda relaxed as her grandmother's

words came back to her. Of course. Mykal and Camille would be there. She wouldn't be alone. They could help her get through whatever waited for them in the wilds of Aquaria.

Zenda gave Luna a small squeeze. "Thanks," she whispered.

She put Luna back down on the pillow, snuggled under the covers, and closed her eyes.

There was nothing to worry about.

Except maybe roaring river rapids. And bugs that bit you while you were sleeping. And people like Alexandra White, who made mean jokes about you all the time.

Zenda drifted off to sleep. But it wasn't a peaceful sleep.

Once again, in her dreams, she began to run . . . .

Cabbages
and
Kings

Zenda's dreams still danced through her mind when she woke up the next morning. The first rays of the morning sun crept through her window. She didn't have to report to the transport center until ten o'clock, but she didn't mind getting up early. There was someone she wanted to see.

After a hasty breakfast of hazelnut muffins smeared with honey and rose petals, Zenda left her green house on the hill and headed toward the Western Woods. Zenda loved being in the woods in the early morning, although she wasn't often up early enough to experience the sensation. At this time of day, Zenda could almost feel the plants waking up to greet the sun, their leaves stretching to feel its rays. Her *kani* allowed her to tap into a low hum of excitement as the woods celebrated a new day dawning, and the feeling was contagious. Zenda didn't have to go far to reach her destination: the Hawthorn Grove. Zenda made her way around the circle of dark green thorn bushes until she found the arch-shaped entrance that had been pruned into them. As she stepped through the bushes, a stone cottage with a thatched roof came into view. Zenda walked up to the door, which had a single eye carved into the dark wood, and knocked.

A tall woman with long, black hair answered, smiling. "Zenda, how nice to see you," she said. "Isn't today the day you leave for your trip?"

"I wanted to say good-bye, Persuaja," Zenda said. "I hope I'm not too early."

"Nonsense," Persuaja said. "I always wake with the birds. It's quite an excellent time to perform psychic work. Do come in."

Zenda followed Persuaja inside. She had only been to the cabin a few times since she had first met the psychic weeks ago, and she still felt like she had yet to see all there was to see there. Drying herbs and crystals hung from the rafters of the cozy, cluttered living room. Tall shelves crowded with rocks, powders, and potions lined every free inch of wall space.

Persuaja and her house were very much alike. Today, the psychic wore a dress made of material in dark, emerald green. Bracelets covered both of her arms, and countless crystals and pouches hung from cords around her neck.

Persuaja led Zenda to her tiny kitchen and motioned for her to sit at the wood table next to the window. A cup of tea, already poured, sat at each end of the table. Persuaja sat across from Zenda and lifted the cup to her lips. Zenda picked up her tea cup, then realized something. The table had been set with two cups—before Zenda had arrived.

"How did you—" Zenda began, but then stopped herself. Persuaja was gifted with pretty incredible psychic powers. They had met the night Zenda had taken a rare and dangerous orchid from her parents' greenhouse in an attempt to get her gazing ball back. Persuaja had sensed the orchid in the auric field and had come to help Zenda. They had been friends ever since.

Persuaja's dark eyes stared into Zenda's blue ones as she sipped her tea. Finally, Persuaja spoke.

"Something haunts you this morning, Zenda," Persuaja said. "Something from your dreams."

Zenda nodded. "You must know about dreams, right?" she asked. "I've heard that the things you see in your dreams can mean something. Granny Delphie used to say if you dreamed about cabbage, it meant you wouldn't get sick."

Persuaja nodded. "The old folk beliefs. To dream of a badger means long life. To dream of a king means a visit from someone important. There is something to them. Then again, sometimes a king is just a king, and a cabbage is just a cabbage."

Persuaja leaned closer to Zenda. "And sometimes, our dreams are our mind's way of working out worries."

The psychic's words echoed the words of Zenda's mother. Deep down, she knew both women were right. A small part of her had hoped that Persuaja might have some other explanation for her—something to put her at ease.

"You don't have any potion that makes dreams go away, do you?" Zenda asked.

Persuaja gave Zenda a small smile. "I think you know the answer to that, Zenda. Your dream is a part of you. If I made your dream go away, that would leave you less than the person you are. We don't want that, do we?"

Zenda sighed. "No," she said. "I just wish I wasn't so nervous."

"You will do just fine," Persuaja said, standing up. "That is, if you finish your tea and hurry home. You don't want to be late."

Zenda gulped down the tea, which tasted of peppermint and wild berries, and rose from her chair. She knew Persuaja didn't believe in revealing Zenda's future to her, but she had to ask.

"So when you say I'll be fine, is that what you see in the future?"

"No," Persuaja said. She leaned down, and her myriad of bracelets rattled as she gave Zenda a rare hug. "That's what I see in *you.* Now go."

Bad News

"This is so exciting, Zen!" Camille said a few hours later. "I've never been in the transport tunnels before."

Zenda smiled, despite her nervousness. Just a few weeks ago, she had taken the transport tunnels for the first time, too, to visit her cousins on the planet Crystallin. She had been just as excited as Camille was now.

The tunnels were located in the hills just outside of Zenda's village. The transport technology had been developed on Crystallin long ago. But the people of Azureblue had embraced the tunnels for their cleanliness and simplicity. Zenda wasn't exactly sure how they worked—students weren't taught that part until their tenth year of school. She did know that each tunnel acted like a shortcut through time and space to a different place in the solar system. Zenda felt that being in the tunnel was like being in a dream, almost. When you woke up, you found yourself where you were supposed to be.

Zenda, Camille, and Mykal were standing outside the transport station—a low, round, white building—with the rest of their classmates. Everyone was chatting in excited tones about the trip.

"Great Aunt Tess says I used the tunnels with my parents when I was just a baby," Mykal said. "But I don't remember."

Zenda noticed a little sadness in Mykal's tone. Her friend's parents had died a year ago in an accident. He lived with his Great Aunt Tess now, and even though she was wonderful, Zenda knew how much Mykal missed his mother and father. She couldn't imagine what she would do if something happened to Verbena and Vetiver. Thinking of them gave her a sudden pang of anxiety.

"Maybe you'll remember when you go through the tunnels again," Camille said soothingly.

"Maybe," Mykal said.

Zenda decided to change the subject.

"What did you two pack? I wasn't sure what to bring."

Mykal held up his green pack, which had a series of pockets attached to the front.

"A guide to the plants of Aquaria," Mykal said. "You never know when that might be useful. And some herb tinctures, in case anyone gets injured. And a seed collecting kit, of course. Do you know that there are plants on Aquaria that don't grow in the wild on Azureblue?"

Zenda smiled. "Yes, I do, because you've told us both about a thousand times since you found out about the trip," she teased. Camille giggled.

Mykal loved plants more than anyone Zenda knew, except for her own parents. He had been helping out at their karmaceutical company ever since Zenda could remember. Most of the time, plants were all Mykal talked about.

"It's okay, Mykal," Camille said. "I'm

hoping to see some rare bugs on Aquaria too." Camille wanted to be an ethno-entomologist someday—someone who could communicate with insects. "I brought my sketchbook in case I see anything good. And my magnifying glass."

Zenda thought of the contents of her bag, which contained mostly clothes, and felt left out. Mykal and Camille were so lucky to know what they wanted to do with their lives. Zenda wasn't sure at all. *Kani* was a great gift, but Zenda wasn't as crazy about plants as Mykal was.

"I brought my journal," Zenda volunteered. Although she suddenly had no idea how a journal would be useful on a survival trip.

But Mykal seemed excited. "What a great idea," he said. "You can keep a record of everything that happens. So we won't forget."

Zenda felt herself blushing at the compliment. With his shaggy blond hair and emerald green eyes, Zenda had always thought he was one of the cutest boys in the village. And he was definitely the nicest.

"I didn't bring anything as useful as a tincture or a plant guide," she said. She looked down at herself. "I think I wore the right thing, at least."

Zenda almost always wore dresses. But her father had convinced her that some draw-string pants would make more sense on a camping trip. She was glad she had listened to him. All of the other girls were wearing pants of some kind. But even though they weren't wearing dresses, they still all wore a flower crown on their heads. Every young girl on Azureblue wore one.

Zenda had made herself an ivy crown this morning, just to be safe. Whenever she got nervous or angry or experienced some other strong emotion, her *kani* would cause the flowers on her crown to change color or fall off or something else equally embarrassing. She didn't want to take any chances, and the simple green leaves of the ivy seemed harmless enough. The color contrasted nicely with her purple shirt and pants.

Camille wore a crown of bright yellow bee flowers that shone like the sun in her black hair. She wore a matching shirt and a pair of loose cotton pants in a soft green.

Then the sound of clapping rose up, drowning out the voices of the students. Zenda looked up to see Wei Lan, the head-master of the Cobalt School for Boys, calling for everyone's attention. The boys and girls immediately quieted down. There was some-thing about Wei Lan's crisp, calm demeanor that was difficult to ignore.

"It is almost time for us to transport," he said. "I would like the boys to gather around me and the girls to gather around Marion Rose, please. We have a few words to say before we begin this exciting journey."

Zenda and Camille left Mykal and

walked over to Marion Rose, the teacher of the seventh-year girls. Zenda was secretly glad that Magenta White, the headmistress of the Cobalt School for Girls, hadn't gone on the trip instead. Marion Rose was much more friendly and approachable. And it didn't help that Magenta White was Alexandra's mother.

The teacher beamed at the girls, a smile on her round face. As usual, she had her thick blonde hair pulled back in a long braid. She wore a green shirt underneath a pair of brown overalls.

"We are going to have so much fun on this trip!" she said in her usual cheerful voice. "Before we get to Aquaria, I'm going to give you your tent assignments. Once you transport, please group together with your tent partners. You'll need to work together right away to get your tents set up."

Marion Rose began reading off names. Zenda listened until she heard, "And our next group is Zenda, Camille . . ."

Zenda and Camille looked at each other and smiled.

". . . Sophia . . ."

Zenda's smile got bigger. Sophia was one of the nicest girls in the class.

" . . . and Alexandra."

Zenda froze. Had she heard right?

Camping on Aquaria was going to be challenging enough. How was she supposed to share a tent with her worst enemy?

# Into the Woods

A few feet away, Zenda heard a loud groan. It came from Alexandra, of course. She wasn't any more pleased about the news than Zenda.

"Marion Rose, can't I go in another tent?" Alexandra complained.

Marion Rose shook her head. "That's the plan, Alexandra. And for the next two days, it's very important that we all stick to the plan. There are real dangers on Aquaria."

"But isn't Zenda's *kani* dangerous too?" Alexandra asked in an innocent-sounding voice. "For all we know, she could make some strange Aquarian plant explode, like she did with those firebrush flowers. It's not safe to be in a tent with her."

Some of the girls laughed, and Zenda felt her cheeks burn. It was true. Her *kani* had made some flowers explode—in front of everyone in both schools. But nobody else except Alexandra was mean enough to remind her of it.

"Zenda is no danger to anyone," Marion Rose said, the cheerfulness gone from her voice. "I think you owe her an apology."

Alexandra gave Zenda a big, fake smile. "Sorry, Zenda," she said in a voice that said exactly the opposite.

"Don't worry about her," Camille whispered in Zenda's ear.

But Zenda felt more worried than ever. Sharing a tent with Alexandra was the worst thing she could imagine.

A girl wearing a pair of paint-splattered overalls walked up. "I'm glad to be in a tent with you two," Sophia said. Then she lowered her voice to a whisper. "Not so glad about Alexandra, though. Do you think we should put a frog in her bed pack tonight? I hear there are lots of frogs on Aquaria."

Camille and Zenda laughed, and Zenda immediately felt better. Delphina's wise words about friends came back to her again. Having Camille and Sophia in the tent would certainly make things easier.

Marion Rose finished calling out tent assignments. "Line up please, girls," she said. "It's time to transport!"

Zenda, Camille, and Sophia ended up in back of the line. Up ahead, Zenda could see Alexandra's head of long, chestnut hair, and her stomach knotted again. She took a deep breath and followed the rest of the students as they filed inside the transport station.

The walls inside the station were lined with doors marked with the names of planets and Azureblue's four moons. Two doors were marked "Aquaria." The boys lined up in front of one, and the girls lined up in front of the other.

Wei Lan and Marion Rose went first. Men and women in white uniforms monitored the lines, giving instructions and making sure the students didn't stray.

Mykal was ahead of them on the boys' line. He turned and waved before entering the marked door. A few minutes later, it was Camille's turn. She gave Zenda's hand a squeeze.

"Are you sure it doesn't hurt?" she asked Zenda.

"Not a bit," Zenda said. "You just might get a little dizzy."

Camille nodded. "See you on Aquaria!"

A minute or two passed, and then a woman attendant opened the door up again. The chamber inside was empty.

"Your turn," she said, smiling. "Have you done this before?"

Zenda nodded. "Not long ago," she said. She stepped through the door and placed her feet on a silver square in the center of the narrow, white-walled chamber. The attendant smiled.

"Keep your hands at your sides, and enjoy the trip," she said.

The woman closed the door. Just as Zenda remembered, a clear tube rose up from the floor, encircling her. Zenda looked up. There was no ceiling above her, only a mass of sky and stars.

And then everything changed, and Zenda felt like her whole body turned to liquid. Rainbow colors swirled in the darkness around her.

And then as suddenly as it had started, the strangeness stopped. Zenda found herself in a white chamber again. The tube descended, and the door opened in front of her.

Zenda stepped out onto a smooth, rocky platform. Girls and boys were gathered around piles of equipment. Camille came running up to her.

"Zenda! That was so amazing! And it didn't hurt at all!" she cried.

Sophia waved them over. "Hey! Our tent stuff is over here!"

Spread across the ground in front of Sophia were four bedrolls, a long tent in a canvas bag, and another knapsack with some

31

tools hanging off of it.

"Each group is responsible for carrying its own equipment," Marion Rose called out. "Once everyone transports, we'll hike to our campsite."

Alexandra was standing off to the side with her two best friends, tall, dark Gena and petite, light-haired Astrid. She rolled her eyes. Then she sighed and stomped toward Zenda and Camille and Sophia. Without saying a word, she picked up one of the bedrolls. Then she walked back to her friends.

Zenda knew it wasn't worth saying anything. She picked up one end of the tent.

"Who wants the other end?" she asked.

"Me!" Camille cried.

"I'll take the backpack," Sophia said. She hoisted it onto her back, pushing her curly brown hair out of the way.

Soon everyone was ready to go. Marion Rose led the girls first. They marched away from the transport station, and Zenda suddenly realized she wasn't on Azureblue anymore.

When she had visited Crystallin, she had truly felt like she was on another world. Its rocky, barren landscape looked nothing like Azureblue, which was filled with trees and plants.

Aquaria was just as green as her home planet, but to Zenda it seemed much, much more wild. On Azureblue, the plant life was interspersed among neatly kept dirt paths or marked off by wood fences. A neat stone wall surrounded the forest, and Zenda's own village was blanketed by fields of herbs and flowers growing in neat rows.

But as far as Zenda could see, nothing looked neat on Aquaria. The trees and plants looked larger, and they grew in every direction, with no boundaries. Everything seemed rugged and untamed, and for a moment, the sensation made Zenda feel light-headed.

*So much life*, Zenda realized. *So wild and free.*

Marion Rose led them off of the rocky platform and down a small hill until they reached the bank of a wide, raging river. Forest surrounded the river on both sides.

"Aquaria has nearly fifty times more rivers, lakes, and streams than Azureblue," Marion Rose explained as they walked. "We'll follow this river to our campsite. If we keep to the river, we can't get lost."

The river was much larger and moved much more swiftly than the peaceful waters of Crystal Creek as it flowed through their village. Zenda wondered if that was why the air around them smelled so clean and bright.

The dirt underneath their feet was worn down by the feet of previous travelers, and in less than an hour, they came upon a large clearing on the river's edge. Marion Rose set down the tent she was carrying.

"We'll set up on the north side of camp, and the boys will set up on the south side," Marion Rose said. "Is there anyone who can tell me where north is?"

Zenda searched her brain for the answer. Marion Rose had given them several lessons on surviving Aquaria before they had arrived. But she couldn't remember a thing.

Another girl raised her hand. "Ciro is visible in the sky in the north, right?" she asked.

Marion Rose smiled. "Good job! Now find north and get your tents set up. You'll find instructions inside the tent covers."

Zenda scanned the sky and found Ciro, the largest of Azureblue's four moons, hanging over the treetops bordering the back of the clearing. It was clearly visible against the blue sky.

She, Camille, and Sophia wandered off toward the trees. Sophia pointed in the distance.

"It looks like nice, smooth ground over there," she said.

"Sounds good to me," Zenda said. She

and Camille followed Sophia.

"Back home, my mom and I go camping in the woods all the time," Sophia explained as she walked. "It's not really that hard."

When they came to the smooth spot, Sophia set the backpack on the ground. Zenda and Camille dropped the tent. Camille opened the cover and pulled out several long poles and a rolled-up piece of canvas. A piece of paper fluttered out and landed on the ground. Zenda picked it up.

She groaned. The paper had written instructions for setting up the tent, along with diagrams, but it all looked like a bunch of lines and arrows to Zenda.

Sophia smiled. "It's not as hard as it looks," she said. "Why don't you go look for some vines to secure the tent poles, and Camille and I will get started?"

"Sure," Zenda said, relieved. Finding vines was something she could do.

Camille was frowning. "Isn't Alexandra

supposed to be helping us?" she asked.

Zenda scanned the crowd of girls and saw Alexandra sitting under a tree, talking with Gena and Astrid.

Sophia shrugged. "She wouldn't be much help, anyway. We can do a better job without her."

Zenda headed off into the trees. As she stepped under the shadow of the branches, everything suddenly became quieter and darker.

Zenda normally felt comfortable in the calm, quiet woods back home, but the Aquarian woods seemed different somehow. Stranger. The trees seemed taller; their branches seemed to reach down, as though they might grab her at any second. Zenda thought of the dark woods in her dream, and she shuddered.

*Focus*, she told herself. *All you have to do is get some vines. You can do that!*

It didn't take long to find some good,

strong vines wrapped around a tree trunk nearby. Zenda unwrapped the vines and then gently coaxed them off the tree, using a little of her *kani*. The vines coiled neatly in her open arms.

Zenda felt relieved, eager to get back in the sunlight. She started to walk back toward the clearing.

But the memory of her dream lingered, and all the fear from the night before flooded back. What if they couldn't put up the tent? What if Marion Rose expected them to swim in that wide, fast river? What if Alexandra White kept saying mean things? What if Zenda got lost in the woods, trapped in the embrace of the tall trees, and never went home to Azureblue again?

Zenda could feel the vines shift and writhe in her arms. Her nervous energy was reaching the plants through her *kani*, she knew. But she couldn't control it.

Zenda ran through the woods until she

reached the clearing. She found Sophia and Camille setting up the tent poles.

"I've got the vines," Zenda said, tossing them onto the ground.

But thanks to Zenda's anxiousness, the vines had come to life. They whirled around the tent poles like angry snakes. The poles came crashing down. Zenda watched, helpless, as one fell on Sophia and sent her sprawling onto the ground.

"Sophia!" Zenda cried.

Behind her, she heard Alexandra's smug voice.

"I told you Zenda was dangerous!"

Wild Things

Marion Rose walked over. "What's going on?"

Zenda felt awful. "It was the vines," she said. "They started to move around, and then the tent came down, and Sophia—"

"I'm fine," Sophia said, standing up. She winced as she set her left ankle on the ground.

Marion Rose knelt down and examined Sophia's ankle. "It's twisted," she said. "I've got a first-aid kit. We'll get that wrapped up."

Alexandra's dark eyes flashed. "You cannot expect me to share a tent with Zenda after this!" she said indignantly. "When my mother hears about this—"

"Your mother is the one who made the tent assignments," Marion Rose replied firmly. "Zenda did not do this on purpose, I am sure."

"No!" Zenda said quickly. "It just happened. I'm so sorry."

Sophia nodded sympathetically, but Zenda could see her face grimace with pain. "I know Zenda didn't do it on purpose. If I'm not

41

afraid to stay in a tent with Zenda, then Alexandra shouldn't be, either."

Alexandra looked furious. "But—"

"This discussion is over," Marion Rose said. "Sophia, come with me. The rest of you, finish setting up the tent. I want all of you working together."

Marion Rose put an arm around Sophia and they walked away, Sophia hopping on one foot. Alexandra rudely grabbed the directions out of Camille's hands.

"I might as well make sure this gets done right," she snapped. "Camille, pick up that pole over there!"

Camille immediately did as she was told. Zenda knew her shy friend would never stand up to bossy Alexandra. She might have tried herself, but she was feeling too bad about Sophia. She almost felt she deserved to be yelled at. She let Alexandra order her and Camille around until the tent was put together.

Marion Rose and Sophia came back just as they finished.

"Nice work," Marion Rose admired.

"If they had asked me for my help to begin with, maybe Sophia wouldn't have gotten hurt," Alexandra replied. Zenda glared at her, remembering how Alexandra had sat chatting with her friends instead of helping like she was supposed to. But she said nothing.

When they had pitched all of the tents, Marion Rose and Wei Lan called the boys and girls together in the center of the clearing.

"We'll spend the rest of the morning looking for food," Marion Rose announced. "Then, this afternoon, we're going to go rafting down the river and then hike back up to camp."

"The more food you find, the more energy you'll have for the trip," Wei Lan said, his eyes twinkling.

"What if we don't find any food? Will

we starve out here?" one of the boys called out. Zenda had been thinking the same thing.

"We have extra provisions, of course," Wei Lan explained. "But I think you may be surprised at how plentiful the wild food is here."

Marion Rose went on to explain the best places to look for wild things to eat: leafy plants and edible flowers along the water's edge and the trail, berry bushes back near the hillside, nut trees growing on the outskirts of the forest, and ferns growing close to the forest floor. Most residents of Azureblue were taught which wild plants were safe to eat and which were not from a very young age, but the teachers had reviewed the wild plants on Aquaria just before the trip so everyone knew what to look for.

"We're going to divide you into four groups: flowers, nuts, berries, and ferns," Wei Lan explained. "Let's meet back here in an hour and then start lunch."

Marion Rose walked among the girls, giving them their assignments and cloth sacks for carrying back their finds. When she came to Zenda's group, she looked at Camille and Alexandra.

"You two can go join the fern group," she said. "Sophia, you stay here and keep off of your ankle for a while."

Then she turned to Zenda. "Why don't you keep Sophia company?"

Zenda nodded. Deep down, she wondered if Marion Rose was afraid to send her near plants after what had happened. But leaving Sophia alone didn't seem right. It was only fair for Zenda to stay with her.

"Let's sit by the river," Sophia suggested. "The air there feels great, doesn't it?"

Zenda smiled. Sophia was someone Zenda had always liked being around, but didn't know much about. She and Sophia found a grassy spot on the riverbank and sat down, facing the water.

"Hey, Zenda! Aren't you coming?" Mykal's voice cried behind her.

Zenda turned. Mykal was standing with a group of boys and waving to her.

"I'll explain later!" Zenda called back.

Then Alexandra walked up to Mykal. "Didn't you hear? Zenda's *kani* went crazy and she hurt Sophia," she said in a voice loud enough for Zenda to hear. "I'll tell you all about it."

Mykal frowned, and Zenda resisted the urge to walk over and confront Alexandra. What was the point, anyway? It wasn't like Alexandra would ever apologize.

"That girl is so rude," Sophia said beside her. "My mom says it's because she's an only child."

Zenda blushed. "I'm an only child." Did Sophia think she was rude too?

But Sophia smiled back. "Then Mom must be wrong, because you and Alexandra are nothing alike," she said. "I've got four older brothers. When you have a big family, you learn how to get along with other people pretty quickly."

"Four older brothers?" Sophia may as well have said she lived with a herd of elephants. Zenda couldn't imagine sharing her house with four boys.

"They're all right," Sophia replied. "At least I get my own room."

A small red bird with yellow markings on its wings flew past them, alighting on top of a tall reed growing out of the river. The girls stopped talking as they watched the bird balance on top of the reed, swaying gently back and forth. The bird let out a high-pitched chirp, then flew off.

"That was so pretty," Zenda remarked.

"I know," agreed Sophia. "Red's my favorite color."

"Mine's purple," Zenda replied.

Sophia grinned. "Red and purple look good together, don't you think? What's your favorite food?"

Zenda thought, but couldn't come up with an answer. She loved everything her father cooked for her. "I'm not sure."

"I *love* hot peppers," Sophia said enthusiastically. "I could eat them on everything! I don't think they grow any on Aquaria, though." Sophia patted her stomach. "I'm hungry! I don't know how Marion Rose and Wei Lan expect us to survive on nuts and berries."

As much as Zenda liked nuts and berries, it didn't sound like a filling meal. "I guess we'll have to see what everyone brings back."

They didn't have to wait long, because groups of students started returning to the clearing, their cloth sacks stuffed. Zenda and Sophia left the riverbank to see what everyone had found.

The nut group came back first, their sacks filled with chestnuts and hazelnuts. The flower group came back with sacks of bright yellow helia flowers that had been dug up to keep their underground tubers intact; tall, green stalks of cattails; and a mound of young dandelions. The berry group's sacks were stained purple from the blackberries that the students had gathered.

Alexandra had gone with the berry group, and when she returned, Zenda noticed that she wore a different flower crown this time. So did some of the other girls.

"Alexandra, are those rowan leaves?" someone asked her.

"Of course," Alexandra replied in a loud voice. "For protection, of course."

Zenda knew what was coming next.

Alexandra looked right at Zenda. "If Marion Rose won't move me to a different tent, I have to do what I can to protect myself." She paused dramatically. "Before I become Zenda's next victim!"

*Rapids*

Thankfully, Zenda saw Camille and Mykal emerge from the forest with the other members of the fern group. Her friends ran up and Mykal opened up his sack to reveal young green fern heads, their fronds curled up into spirals.

"We found so many," Mykal said, his voice filled with excitement. "Everything grows so well here. Bigger than on Azureblue too."

"And I saw a moss worm," Camille added. "A genuine Aquarian moss worm!"

Zenda wanted to ask what a genuine Aquarian moss worm looked like, but Marion Rose and Wei Lan immediately put everyone to work. The teachers built two fires and set out pots, pans, and other cooking supplies. Some students were sent to the river to wash the cattails and peel off the outer green layer to reveal a whitish core underneath. Others rinsed and plucked off dandelion leaves, or washed and peeled the round, bumpy tubers of the helia flowers.

Zenda and Sophia joined the fern group, who were given the task of cooking the fern heads in pans of boiling water over the fire. When the ferns were tender, Marion Rose gave them some oil and told them to cook the ferns in the oil this time, until they were crisp.

When everyone was done, each student had a full, heaping plate of food. Zenda couldn't believe how delicious everything was. The cattails had been sliced and boiled and served with salt and pepper. The tubers of the helia flowers had been boiled and mashed and tasted just like potatoes! The dandelion leaves made a nice salad. And Zenda's favorite, not just because she had helped, were the fried fern heads.

"This isn't bad," Sophia said, cleaning the last bite from her plate.

"Not bad?" Mykal said. "It's the best meal I've ever had!" He jumped to his feet and went back for seconds.

By the time they cleaned up the camp-site, the sun was shining high over Aquaria. Marion Rose and Wei Lan gathered everyone by the river to start their rafting trip.

Since they would only be rafting a short way down the river, and then spending some time in the woods before hiking back up, the teachers had encouraged everyone to bring along items they could use to explore the nature they found. Zenda slipped her journal into a small pouch and slung it over her shoulders. Camille packed her magnifying glass and her sketchbook, and was happy to see that Sophia had one too. Alexandra didn't pack anything.

"We can see plants every day on Azureblue," she said, shrugging. "I don't see what the big deal is."

A series of rafts lined the riverbank. The inflated rafts were long, with rounded edges and made of a heavy canvas material.

"There will be four boys and four girls in

each raft," Wei Lan explained. "Marion Rose will assign each tent to a raft."

Zenda beamed when her teacher grouped the girls in her tent with Mykal and three other boys: Torin, a short boy with a mop of brown hair and big, brown eyes; Ferris, a tall, thin boy with red hair; and Darius, who had short, dark hair, skin the color of a ripe acorn, and one of the nicest smiles Zenda had ever seen.

Ferris jumped in their raft first and grabbed an oar. "Let's ride the rapids!" he yelled.

Wei Lan approached, shaking his head. "First, we must put the rafts in the water," he advised.

"Sure," Ferris said, grinning widely.

Mykal gave Zenda a secret smile as Ferris climbed out of the raft. Following Wei Lan's instructions, they brought the raft to the water's edge. Then they waded in a few feet before climbing aboard.

Each raft had four oars, and the boys immediately grabbed theirs.

"No fair," Sophia said. "I want to row too."

Mykal immediately gave Sophia his oar. Torin turned and gave Zenda a shy smile.

"You can have mine if you want," he said.

"No, thanks," Zenda said quickly. She had no idea what to do with the oar—except maybe to look silly in front of everyone.

"Come on," Torin urged. "You should try."

Zenda knew Torin wouldn't take no for an answer. "I'm not sure I even know how to use it," she admitted.

"It's easy," Sophia said. "Just do what I do. Then Camille and Alexandra can take turns."

Zenda gave in. "Okay," she said, taking the oar from Torin. She watched Sophia to see how she was gripping the oar—one hand in front of the handle, the other behind it.

They each took a position around the perimeter of the raft and sat down. Then, at Wei Lan's cue, they began to paddle around the river.

Although the river was flowing swiftly, the raft floated smoothly over the surface of the water. Zenda followed Sophia's cue and pushed the oar through the water with short, clean strokes.

"One, two! One, two!" Ferris called out, keeping time.

After a few minutes, Zenda realized she was actually enjoying herself. She was paddling the raft! She could do it! The sky was bright, the air was clear, and the trees they passed as they floated down the river were beautiful. Before she knew it, Marion Rose was calling to them to paddle toward the shore.

"The river dips up ahead, and gets much faster," she called out. "Just start paddling as hard as you can, and you'll be fine!"

Zenda felt something yank at her oar.

"I haven't had a turn yet," Alexandra complained.

"Fine," Zenda said. As she turned to hand Alexandra the oar, Alexandra grabbed it from her with a jerk.

The raft lurched violently. Alexandra fell backward, knocking into Mykal and Camille.

The sudden movement sent the raft spiraling in the water.

"Hey!" Ferris yelled. "We're losing control!"

The swift current carried the raft down the river, turning in circles. Ferris, Darius, and Sophia paddled frantically, but it didn't do any good. The raft slammed into three tall rocks jutting out of the middle of the river.

Then it stopped. The rocks formed a tight wedge around the raft, trapping it.

"Push out!" Sophia cried. She pressed

her oar against one of the rocks and tried to push back. Ferris and Darius did the same. But the raft wouldn't budge.

"How do we get out of this?" Camille asked nervously.

Zenda was worried too. To the right, she could see the other rafts landing smoothly on the shore. But just past the rocks, the river dipped sharply, creating a small, fast waterfall.

"Just keep pushing!" Sophia cried.

Ferris dropped his oar in the bottom of the raft. "Forget it," he said. "I'm going for a swim."

With a yell, Ferris jumped off the raft and splashed into the water. Torin and Darius grinned at each other. They jumped in next, whooping loudly.

Marion Rose called out to them from the shore. "You might as well all swim, if you can," she cried. "The water's calm here, but if that raft gets loose, you'll be out of control on the rapids."

Mykal shrugged. "I guess we might as well." He turned to Sophia. "How's your ankle?"

"I can swim," Sophia said. "Don't worry about me." With that, she jumped into the water.

Zenda moved to join her, but stopped. She realized she didn't have her shoulder pouch.

"Looking for this?" Alexandra asked. She held up the pouch by its strap.

"Thanks," Zenda said. "It must have fallen off when you took the oar."

Alexandra's mouth formed a thin smile. "Here, catch!" she cried.

Alexandra hurled the pouch at least two feet to Zenda's left and far too high to catch. It splashed into the water and disappeared down the rapids.

"Hey!" Zenda cried, standing up. "You did that on purpose!"

At that moment, the raft jolted loose

from the rocks. Zenda and Alexandra both lost their footing and fell backwards into the raft. Mykal and Camille each grabbed an oar and began paddling.

It was no use. The swift current grabbed hold of the raft and sent them hurtling down the waterfall!

*Lost!*

Water splashed into the raft, drenching them as they tumbled down the waterfall. By some miracle, they landed upright at the bottom.

Zenda pulled herself up and grabbed an oar. But Marion Rose had been right. The current in this part of the river was strong — too strong. She and Mykal and Camille paddled furiously, but it didn't do any good. The rapids carried them farther and farther away from the waterfall.

"You're not doing it right!" Alexandra snapped. "There's got to be some way to stop this thing!"

Zenda stopped rowing. "I don't see you doing anything to help!" she retorted. "If you hadn't thrown my pouch into the water, this wouldn't have happened."

Only Mykal and Camille were paddling, and the raft began to spin wildly in circles.

"Can you two stop fighting and start paddling?" Camille pleaded. She sounded very worried. The tone in her friend's voice surprised Zenda, and she immediately put her oar in the water. Alexandra reluctantly picked up an oar too.

With all four of them paddling, the raft straightened out. But they still couldn't control it.

Zenda started to panic. They couldn't even see the waterfall anymore, they had come so far. And, up ahead, the river forked into two directions. She knew it wouldn't matter which way they wanted to go; the river would decide for them.

And the river did. It sent them down the right fork, farther and farther, until the rapids finally slowed down enough for them to get control of the raft.

"Let's try to get her ashore!" Mykal cried.

Zenda paddled with all her might. Slowly, the raft changed direction and they were able to paddle toward the shoreline.

Mykal jumped out first and grabbed the rope on the end of the raft. The girls jumped out next and helped him pull the raft to the shore. When they reached land, Mykal flopped onto the sandy bank, exhausted.

Camille looked shaken. "I'm so glad we landed," she sighed, sitting on a rock.

Alexandra scowled and stood, staring at the water with her arms folded. "Wait until my mother hears about this," she muttered.

Zenda flopped onto the ground next to Mykal. Her arms ached with the effort of paddling. Her clothes clung to her skin, drenched with cold river water.

The four were silent for a moment as the situation sank in. Mykal spoke first.

"I guess we're lost," he said simply.

"No kidding, genius," Alexandra said, rolling her eyes.

*Lost.* Zenda flashed back to her panicked thoughts in the woods this morning.

They were lost on Aquaria. Lost on a

wild, untamed moon with no raft, no equipment, no way of sending a message for help.

Zenda bolted upright, her breath coming in short gasps.

"What are we going to do?" she wailed.

*Lura Berries*

"We get back to the others," Alexandra said. "What else are we supposed to do?"

Zenda looked up at the sky. The sun was already starting to sink over the horizon. They might be able to make it back to camp by following the riverbank, but they had come a long way. Would they make it by nightfall? Surely, they'd never be able to find the others in the dark.

Mykal had the same thought. "It's too late," he said. "We should find some shelter, and maybe some food, so we can be safe for the night."

"Maybe they'll come looking for us," Camille said hopefully.

"Maybe," Mykal said. "But we can't count on that. We should stay right here until the morning."

Zenda struggled to take deep breaths. Mykal sounded so calm. But how could he be? They didn't even have a tent. They'd be out in the open, open to the elements, bugs, and whatever strange creatures came out on Aquaria at night.

"Staying out here all night is a crazy idea," Alexandra snapped. "We should go back now."

"I think we should vote on it," Camille suggested quietly.

"Good idea," Mykal agreed. "If we're going to get through this, we need to start acting like a team."

Camille nodded. "I vote we find shelter for tonight. That's what Marion Rose taught us in class."

"Me too," Mykal said quickly.

Zenda knew they were right. "I vote with them," she said, although the thought of camping in the open terrified her.

Alexandra turned her back to them and stomped off down the riverbank. "Fine," she said, without looking back. "I'll go myself."

Alexandra walked a little ways and then stopped, turned around, and scowled. She must have realized no one was coming after her.

"Fine," she said. "We'll stay here. But I still think you're wrong."

Alexandra stomped back down the bank.

"So," she said snidely. "Should we *vote* on what to do next?"

"We should find someplace to sleep first," Camille said nervously. "I mean, that's what we learned in class, right?"

Mykal scanned the sky. "I don't think it's supposed to rain," he said. "Maybe someplace open, so we can build a fire to keep warm."

It didn't take long before they found an open area covered with low grass about halfway between the riverbank and the forest.

"This looks good," Zenda said, and everyone agreed.

"We'll need a fire," Mykal said.

Camille took her magnifying glass out of her pouch. "We can use this to reflect the light of the sun," she said. "We can start with some pages from my sketchbook."

"We'll need twigs and branches," Mykal said. "Maybe we can look for those and something to eat at the same time."

"That's not a bad idea," Alexandra admitted. "Should we split up?"

"No!" Zenda said quickly. They were lost already. Losing each other would be even worse.

"Fine," Mykal said. "Let's head to the woods."

The floor of the woods was littered with fallen twigs and branches, and Zenda and Camille quickly filled their arms with them. Mykal took out his guidebook to plants on Aquaria and walked while poring through its pages at the same time.

"Maybe there'll be some ferns here," Zenda said hopefully, although she wasn't sure how they would cook them without a frying pan.

"We'll probably find more plants back by the trail," Mykal said. "There are usually some edible things you can find in a forest, but I don't see any ferns here."

Alexandra grabbed the book from his hands. "Let me see that," she said. "There's got to be something to eat around here."

Mykal started to protest, but Camille cried out first. "What's over there?"

Zenda followed Camille's gaze and saw a thick blanket of vines climbing up an oak tree. Clusters of white berries hung from the vines.

"Wow," Mykal said. "I've never seen those before."

Alexandra leafed through the guide-book. Then she stopped and proudly held out a page to show Mykal.

"They're lura berries," she said. "It says here that they're edible, and very high in vitamins, besides."

Mykal leaned over her shoulder. "She's

right," he said.

Alexandra snapped the book shut. "Let's pick them then!"

She reached out and grabbed a cluster. Then she picked a few off and popped them into her mouth.

"Mmm," she said. "Delicious!"

Zenda, Mykal, and Camille each did the same. Zenda cautiously put one of the berries in her mouth. It tasted sweet and earthy at the same time. She ate a few more.

"We should save them for later," Mykal said.

Everyone agreed, and Camille volunteered her cloth pouch as a berry holder. Soon the pouch was full.

They headed back to their campsite, picking up more twigs and branches as they went. They dumped the wood in a pile on the ground.

"Not bad," Mykal said. "Camille, why don't you and Alexandra get a fire going?

Zenda and I will go look for more food."

"I can look for food too," Alexandra said.

"But Zenda's good with plants," Mykal said. "Her *kani* might help us. And we shouldn't leave anybody alone. Zenda and I won't go far."

"We could vote again," Camille suggested, giving Zenda a wink.

"Don't bother," Alexandra said, frowning. "I know how it will turn out. Have fun!"

Mykal held out his hand. "Can I please have my guidebook?"

Alexandra rolled her eyes, but handed it to him. Zenda and Mykal headed toward the riverbank, where they knew they'd be more likely to find green, leafy plants to eat. Sure enough, they found a low-growing plant with wide, green leaves as soon as they reached the shoreline. Mykal looked it up in the guidebook.

"The leaves are edible," he said after a

few moments. "They're supposed to taste like spinach."

Zenda's stomach grumbled. "Do you think there are any chocolate cake plants growing on Aquaria? Or pancake plants?"

Mykal grinned. "It's only one night. I'll get Aunt Tess to make us a chocolate cake when we get home."

Zenda had crouched down to collect the leaves when something caught her eye, floating in the water. Something purple.

Her shoulder pouch! She let out a happy cry and headed out in the water to retrieve it.

"That's weird," Mykal said. "How did it end up here? Exactly where we are?"

Zenda didn't care how it had happened. She pulled out her journal. The edges of the pages were soaked, but the thick, silk-covered cover had kept the inside pages dry.

"I'm so glad I found it!" she exclaimed. She had been keeping track of her thoughts in journals ever since she could remember. This journal told the story of how she had broken her gazing ball, and found her first five musings. She didn't ever want to forget that.

Mykal and Zenda headed back to their campsite with the journal and several bundles of green leaves. They returned to find Camille fanning a small fire.

"That's amazing, Cam!" Zenda said, impressed.

Camille looked up and beamed. "I know," she said. "I can't believe I did it!"

Zenda suddenly realized that she had been so busy looking for food and wood that she had almost forgotten her panic. Things didn't look too bad. They had food. Thanks to Camille, they had fire. It would be morning before they knew it, and they'd find the others. They'd have to!

Mykal spread out the leaves on a patch of grass.

"Oh, boy," Alexandra said in a sarcastic

voice. "Leaves and berries for dinner. Yum!"

Mykal sat down and opened up his guidebook. "Something's bugging me about those lura berries," he said. "I think I've heard of them."

Mykal began to read aloud from the book. "Lura berries are a sweet, edible berry found in the wild only on Aquaria," he read. "The berries are not normally eaten on Azureblue, however, because . . ." he stopped.

"Because what?" Camille asked.

Mykal looked at Zenda. "Because the berries have a strange effect on those with the gift of *kani*," he continued. "*Kani* activates a chemical in the berry that causes dreams to take physical form."

Zenda let the words sink in. She had *kani*. She had eaten the berries.

*A chemical in the berry that causes dreams to take physical form.*

Zenda thought of the shapeless creature in her dreams and let out a gasp.

Alexandra smiled. "Gee, Zenda," she said. "I guess that's bad news for you!"

Don't Fall
Asleep

"You only had a few berries, Zenda," Camille said. "That's nothing to worry about, right?"

Mykal frowned. "The guidebook doesn't say."

"Oh, well," Alexandra said. "I guess we'll find out tonight."

Zenda flashed back to the woods and remembered Alexandra holding the guidebook. She had told them the berries were safe to eat. But had she told them everything?

"You knew about this, didn't you?" Zenda angrily accused. "You had the guidebook in your hands. You let me eat those berries!"

Alexandra's eyes widened innocently. "I didn't know, Zenda, honest. What kind of a person do you think I am?"

Zenda felt like a gate had been opened inside her. Normally, she would have held back, but after everything she had been through — everything *Alexandra* had put her through — she couldn't hold it in any longer.

"Do you really want to know what I think of you?" she asked Alexandra. "I think you're a—"

"It's getting dark!" Mykal interrupted loudly. "We can't spend time fighting now. We've got to make sure we have what we need to survive the night."

Zenda knew Mykal was right. But part of her felt betrayed. Alexandra had known about the berries. She might have put Zenda in danger. Wasn't anyone else angry about that?

But she kept silent.

"I'm not fighting with anybody," Alexandra said. "Zenda's the one who started it."

Zenda grew angry again. "Me? I—" she stopped herself. Getting angry was just what Alexandra wanted her to do. Speaking up for herself was one thing, but she knew if she let Alexandra bait her, she'd end up saying something she'd regret.

"It doesn't matter who started what. We

need to decide what we should do next," Zenda said calmly.

"We should collect more wood for the fire, so we can keep it going all night," Mykal said. "That should keep us warm and safe from any predators."

"Predators?" Camille asked, her brown eyes growing wide.

Zenda had the same thought. Who knew what kind of creatures lurked in the rugged woods of Aquaria?

"I'm sure Marion Rose would have mentioned if there were dangerous animals in this part of Aquaria," Zenda said, trying to sound brave. "But it's a good idea to keep the fire going, just to be safe."

"Sure," Mykal agreed.

"I'll collect wood with you, Mykal," Alexandra said.

Mykal nodded. "Zenda and Camille can keep the fire going while we're gone."

Normally, Zenda would have been upset

to see Alexandra go off with Mykal, but she was so happy to see Alexandra leave just then that she found she didn't mind. She and Camille added some bigger branches to the fire and watched the flames leap higher.

Camille was the first to speak. "I know you're mad at Alexandra," she said. "She hasn't been very nice on this trip, has she?"

"No, she hasn't," Zenda said quickly.

"You have a right to be mad," Camille continued. "But I think Mykal's right. We have to work together now. I'm a little scared, Zen."

Zenda looked at Camille's worried face and all of her anger evaporated. "I'm scared too," she admitted. "I've been scared ever since I found out we were coming here. And now we're lost!"

Camille looked over her shoulder at the woods. "What if there are predators in there?"

"We'll be fine," Zenda said. "The fire will keep us safe. And all we have to do is follow the river to get back to camp tomorrow."

Camille nodded. "I hope so."

Soon Mykal and Alexandra returned with their arms full of more fallen branches. Mykal had a surprise too—a pouch filled with ripe chestnuts.

Zenda found a heavy rock and they used it to crack open the chestnut shells and eat the tasty nuts inside. They ate the leafy plants too, and everyone except Zenda ate the lura berries. By the time they finished eating, the sun had gone down, and Ciro was shining overhead.

"We should take turns watching the fire," Mykal said.

"Don't worry," Zenda said. "I'll watch the fire all night. I'm not going to sleep."

"Zenda, we all need to sleep," Camille said. "We're going to need energy for the walk back tomorrow."

"But I ate the lura berries," she said, avoiding Alexandra's gaze. "What if it only takes a few berries, and my dreams become real?"

Alexandra raised an eyebrow. "What are

you afraid of, Zenda? Exactly what kind of dreams do you have?"

"I'm not afraid," Zenda said quickly. She didn't want to think about the shadowy monster that had been chasing her every night, much less talk about it. "But you never know with dreams, right? We'll be safer if I stay awake."

Mykal frowned. "If you get tired, wake me up," he said. "Camille's right. We all need rest."

"I'll be fine," Zenda insisted.

Even though they were on the ground, with no blankets or pillows, everyone was exhausted from the long day. It wasn't long before Mykal, Camille, and Alexandra fell asleep.

Zenda had left her pouch and her open journal near the fire to dry. She picked up the journal and fished out a pen from her pouch. If she was going to stay awake, she might as well do something to pass the time.

I can't believe everything that has happened! I was worried about the trip to Aquaria, but I never imagined things would end up like this.

Alexandra has been saying mean things ever since we got here. When we went rafting yesterday, she tried to take my oar away from me and the raft went out of control. Then she threw my pouch into the water on purpose! The raft fell down a waterfall and we floated down the river really, really far. We went looking for berries, and Alexandra looked in Mykal's guidebook and told us that lura berries were safe to eat. But she forgot to mention that they aren't safe for people with kani—like me!

I am so mad at Alexandra! But Mykal and Camille are right. We can't fight right now. We have to work together so we can get back to camp safely.

I've got to try to stay awake. That strange presence in my dreams is bad enough. If it ever came to life . . .

I can't think about that. It won't matter, anyway, because I'm not going to sleep tonight. I'm sure Marion Rose or Wei Lan will know what to do tomorrow.

Cosmically yours,
Zenda

Zenda closed her journal and sat watching the fire. She absently tugged at the small silk pouch she wore around her neck.

She had begun wearing the pouch when she broke her gazing ball. The pieces appeared out of thin air, and she wanted to make sure she always had a safe place to keep one if it materialized. At home, she kept the pieces, each engraved with a musing, in a special box.

Zenda had received five musings so far. She had found one on the planet Crystallin: *Mirrors reflect but people shine.* That musing had taught her that being beautiful on the outside wasn't as important as being beautiful on the inside.

Zenda looked at Alexandra's sleeping face. With her long, chestnut hair and big eyes, Alexandra was one of the prettiest girls in the class. So why did she have to be so mean on the inside?

*Mirrors reflect but people shine.* Zenda

hadn't exactly been shining on this trip either, she realized.

*But it's not my fault,* she told herself. *Alexandra always starts it. I've never done anything to her!*

Zenda shook away the thought and turned her head to look at the woods. The trees looked like sleeping giants now. Strange sounds issued from deep within the forest — coos and clucks and whooshes that Zenda couldn't identify. She thought about what Mykal had said about predators and scooted closer to the fire.

The warm flames made her sleepy, and she shook her head to stay awake. She couldn't let that creature in her dreams come to life.

Then again, Zenda thought, could it be any worse than what they were facing? They were lost in a wild place. They might find their way back to camp tomorrow — but, then again, they might not. Maybe no one would ever find them. She'd be stuck on Aquaria, living on nuts and leaves for the rest of her life. Even worse—she'd be stuck with Alexandra!

Worried thoughts drifted through Zenda's head, and her eyelids began to droop. And then she drifted off to sleep . . .

*Whirroo!*

*Zenda ran and ran until she couldn't run anymore. She reached the edge of the cliff and spun around.*

*She could see it now. A giant, shadowy form that seemed to be made of dark, spinning clouds. What did it want with her?*

*The being got closer and closer, floating above the ground like some kind of specter. Zenda took a step back . . . and the sound of screaming filled the air.*

Zenda woke with a start. The scream pierced the air—and she wasn't dreaming anymore. As she rubbed the sleep from her eyes, she realized the scream was coming from Alexandra.

Alexandra sat up, propped up on her elbows. She was staring, wide-eyed, at a ball of round fluff on her stomach.

"Get it off me!" Alexandra cried.

Mykal and Camille woke up next.

"What's wrong?" Mykal asked.

"A wild animal! There's a wild animal on

me!" Alexandra shrieked.

Wild animal? The early morning light was dim, but all Zenda could make out was the ball of fur on Alexandra's stomach.

"Jump up!" Camille suggested.

Alexandra scrambled to her feet and ran next to Mykal. The ball of fur tumbled to the ground and rolled in the grass. It made a noise that sounded something like, *"Whirroo! Whirroo!"*

Zenda, Mykal, and Camille took a few cautious steps closer to the fur ball. As Zenda knelt down, the ball stopped rolling. Through the fur, Zenda could make out two shiny black eyes and a tiny snout.

"It's cute!" Camille cried.

"Looks can be deceiving," Alexandra said. "It's probably some kind of flesh-eating Aquarian beast."

*"Whirroo!"* the creature chirped again.

"Mykal, can't you look it up in your guidebook?" Alexandra asked.

"I only brought a plant guidebook," Mykal replied.

"And I only studied Aquarian insects before I came here," Camille said. "I don't think this little guy is an insect."

Something about the creature was familiar to Zenda. Then she remembered a long-buried memory.

"Did any of you ever hear the story of the whirries?" Zenda asked. "Granny Delphie used to tell it to me when I was little. It was about these little furry creatures that lived on the moon and rolled around to get from place to place. If you catch them, they're supposed to grant your wishes. In the story, a fox catches one, but the whirries trick the fox and it gets away."

The look of terror on Alexandra's face softened. "My grandma told me that story too."

"So you think this is a whirrie?" Camille asked. "Maybe it will grant our wishes!"

Camille reached down to pick it up, but the furry creature began quickly to roll away. In a flash, it disappeared into the woods.

Camille frowned. "Too bad. But it did come to you, Alexandra. Maybe if you make a wish, it will come true."

"That's impossible," Alexandra said. "Because my only wish right now is to be back home and as far away from here as possible."

Then Alexandra looked at Zenda, and her eyes narrowed. "Weren't you supposed to be keeping watch? How did that little rat end up on me in the first place? Did you fall asleep? I see you let the fire go out."

Zenda hated to admit the truth. "I think I drifted off," she said.

"I knew it!" Alexandra cried. "We never should have trusted you to stand guard. It's a good thing the only thing that found us was that little whirrie. We could have gotten eaten by an Aquarian grizzly bear or bitten by snakes or something. As it is, I probably got

94

fleas from that thing."

"There are no fleas on Aquaria," Camille said quickly.

"It doesn't matter, because we're all fine," Mykal said. "And it's a good thing Zenda woke us up early. We need to find our way back to camp."

But Alexandra wasn't satisfied. "How do you know that the whirrie thing didn't come from a dream Zenda had?" she asked accusingly. "She probably dreamed about it on purpose so it would attack me!"

"Don't be silly. It didn't attack you," Camille said.

Zenda bit her lip. She didn't want to lie, but she didn't want to worry everyone, either. "I didn't dream about the whirrie," she said. "I didn't have any dreams at all."

"Zenda wouldn't lie," Mykal said firmly. "So that's settled. Let's get moving."

Being next to the river made it easy for them to wash up and get a drink. The river water was icy cold, but very clean.

They ate the rest of the nuts and berries for breakfast (Zenda only ate the nuts, of course), and then started their journey back up the river.

The trail from the transport center to the campsite had been well worn, but this trail was much less traveled. They scrambled over slippery rocks and pushed their way through tall weeds, all the while sticking close to the riverbank.

"I wonder how far we have to go?" Camille asked.

"It's hard to tell," Mykal said. "The raft was moving so fast. It's like it was all a blur."

"It can't be *too* far," Zenda said hopefully.

"It better not be," Alexandra said. "I don't want to spend another night in the wild again. Especially after what happened last night."

Zenda turned to Alexandra, her blue eyes flashing. "What do you mean by that?"

"You know what I mean," Alexandra said. "Falling asleep like that was dangerous. What if you had dreamed about a scary monster or something? We'd all be monster chow by now."

"But we're not, right?" Camille interjected.

Zenda didn't say anything. She marched just up ahead of the group, fuming. Camille stepped up beside her.

"It's not fair," Zenda said. "I'm not doing anything. Why can't she leave me alone?"

"Just ignore her," Camille said. "We'll be back at camp soon."

Mykal and Alexandra came up behind them.

"See any sign of the others?" Mykal asked.

"Nothing but trees and river," Zenda responded.

Mykal shaded his face with his hands and looked up ahead. "I thought by now we'd at least be by that waterfall. But I guess we've got farther to go."

They walked on in silence for a while longer. Then Mykal's face lit up.

"Do you see somebody?" Zenda asked.

"It's a red marshflower," he said, pointing to a clump of plants down at the very edge of the water. "They only grow red on Aquaria."

Mykal scrambled down the riverbank toward the plants. Suddenly, he cried out and came running back up the bank.

"I think I stepped on something," he said. "Some kind of nest."

Before he could explain further, a loud buzzing sound came from the river's edge. A blue cloud lifted off of the ground and floated toward them. As the cloud got closer, Zenda realized it wasn't a cloud at all.

It was a swarm of insects.

Camille's eyes grew wide. "Blue stingers!" she cried. "Everybody get down, quick!"

*Blue Stingers*

Zenda dropped to the ground. She saw Mykal and Camille fall next to her. But where was Alexandra?

Then she heard Alexandra scream. Zenda raised her head. Alexandra was running up the river, surrounded by the swarming blue stingers.

"Alexandra, get down!" Camille yelled. "Blue stingers are sensitive to motion. If you don't move, they won't sting you!"

Alexandra listened this time. She fell to the ground, covering her face with her arms.

The blue stingers buzzed over her body for a few more seconds. Then the cloud of insects headed back to the water. Zenda watched, holding her breath, until the swarm settled down again.

"Is it safe now?" Zenda whispered.

"I think so," Camille said.

They rose to their feet and ran to Alexandra, who was still lying on the ground. She sat up, groaning. There were several nasty, red bumps on her neck and arms.

Zenda grimaced. "Did they sting you?"

Alexandra nodded. Zenda could see tears in her eyes.

"Camille, do you know what do to for blue stinger stings?" Mykal asked.

Camille closed her eyes, thinking. "I should know this," she said. "I think some plant nectars are good, if they have a lot of sugar in them."

Mykal looked through the index of his plant guide, then began leafing through the pages.

"Are there any pea blossoms around here?" he asked. "They've got spiky leaves and small blue flowers and grow near the river. They might work."

"I'll go look," Zenda said. She ran toward the water, being sure to steer clear of the marshflowers. She scanned the riverbank, looking for anything with blue flowers on it.

And then she saw it—spiky leaves, blue

flowers. But it wasn't growing near the river. The plant was growing *in* the river. Its tall stems rose above the swiftly moving current.

"Mykal," Zenda called back. "I think I see them." She pointed toward the plant.

"That's it," Mykal said. "Can you reach it?"

Zenda frowned. Swimming was out of the question because the current was moving far too quickly. She cautiously stepped out onto a flat rock in the shallowest part of the water and reached out. But the flowers were still too far away.

Camille had climbed down to the shore. "Be careful, Zenda!" she called out.

Zenda closed her eyes. The plant was *almost* close enough to touch. If it would just bend toward her a little bit . . .

Zenda had to try to use her *kani*. In the past, she had always been able to touch the plant she was communicating with. She didn't know if she could do it from a distance. But she had to try.

*Please*, Zenda silently pleaded. *My friend is hurt. We need your nectar. If you could just move a little closer.*

Zenda opened her eyes. The clump of pea blossoms began to sway back and forth.

*That's it*, Zenda coaxed. *Come a little closer. You can do it.*

Zenda held her breath as the plant leaned toward her. She reached out, touching her fingertips to the blossoms.

*Thank you*, Zenda told the plant. *Thank you so much.*

The plant leaned all the way into her palm, and Zenda gently plucked off the blue blossoms. Then she exhaled and let go of the plant. It gently sprang back.

Zenda carefully stepped from the rock to the shore. She and Camille climbed up the riverbank. Alexandra's face showed how much pain she was in, and Zenda genuinely felt sorry for her. She opened her palm and showed the blossoms to Mykal.

Mykal gingerly picked up one of the blossoms. The nectar was stored in a tiny pouch underneath the petals. He pressed the petal against one of Alexandra's stings and squeezed out the nectar.

She smiled a little. "It feels better."

Mykal nodded. One by one, he applied nectar to her stings. Zenda could see that the redness lightened a few seconds after the nectar was applied.

"Thank you," Alexandra said weakly. "I don't know why I ran. I guess I panicked."

"I would have run too, if I hadn't read a whole chapter on blue stingers just last week," Camille said.

"Are you okay to walk?" Mykal asked.

Alexandra nodded and got to her feet. "I think so."

Mykal turned to Zenda. "I saw you use your *kani* on that plant. That was really cool."

"Yeah," Alexandra said. "Thanks."

Zenda smiled. It felt good to know her *kani* had helped somebody—even Alexandra. And she was being nice about it, besides.

They continued to walk upriver. Camille and Zenda walked in front side by side.

"That was pretty scary back there," Zenda remarked.

"I know," Camille said. "But we got through it. It got me thinking about how nervous we were about coming here. But I think we're doing pretty great."

Camille smiled, and Zenda smiled back. Camille might be right. For the first time, Zenda began to feel like they would get back to the campsite safely. Everything would be just fine.

Suddenly, a strange noise rose up behind them. It sounded like a howling wind.

"What was that?" Mykal asked. All four of them turned and looked behind them.

A huge, gray cloud was floating across the ground, headed right toward them.

Alexandra let out a little cry. "More blue stingers?"

But Zenda knew it wasn't a swarm of insects headed their way.

The strange being from her dreams had come to life!

Facing Fear

"Those aren't blue stingers," Camille said.

"No," Zenda said. "It's from my dream."

"What happens in the dream?" Mykal asked.

"I run!" Zenda said.

The shapeless, swirling mass was getting closer and closer. It wasn't like it was particularly scary-looking, Zenda realized. But something about it filled her with unspeakable fear and dread.

The others must have felt it too.

"Running sounds good to me," Alexandra said. Without a word, they all turned and charged ahead.

The trail was rocky and full of weeds, making it impossible to run quickly. Zenda could almost feel the presence of the creature behind her. The closer it got, the more frightened she became.

Zenda broke off from the riverbank and headed for open ground on the left. The land sloped uphill, but it was easier than stumbling over the rocky path.

She heard the sound of pounding foot-steps behind her and realized the others had followed her. Zenda felt terrible. She had fallen asleep, and now her friends were in danger.

Zenda quickly looked behind her. Mykal, Camille, and Alexandra weren't far behind. The creature was even closer now, and it seemed to be getting larger.

Zenda quickly scanned the area. Open ground was too dangerous. Maybe they could hide from it—or lose it somehow.

The woods. She changed direction and headed for the tall trees.

"In here!" Zenda cried out.

They all ran into the cover of the trees. As Zenda darted among them, she could hear Mykal, Camille, and Alexandra crashing through the brush behind her.

Zenda looked behind her. She could see her friends, but there was no sign of the creature. Good. Maybe her plan had worked.

Mykal caught up to her. "Zenda, how does your dream end?"

"I keep running," Zenda answered, breathless. "Until I come to something — I think it's a cliff."

As soon as she said the word, the trees parted, and Zenda found herself on the edge of a precipice. She looked down to see a pool of water hundreds of feet below.

She looked back to see the others staring at her with shocked faces.

"What happens when you get to the cliff?" Mykal asked.

"I wake up," Zenda said. "But maybe it's okay. I think we lost it — "

Then she heard the howling, whooshing sound once more. She couldn't see the creature through the trees, but it sounded like it was catching up. Zenda's heart pounded frantically in her chest.

"Think, Zenda," Mykal said. "This came

from your dreams. There's got to be some way to get rid of it."

"I don't know!" Zenda said, her voice rising. "I don't even know what it is. My mom said that sometimes things we're worried about show up in dreams, but—"

"Maybe that's it!" Camille cried. "You were afraid of coming to Aquaria. But you don't have to be afraid anymore. You can survive here. We all can."

"But we're still lost!" Zenda protested.

The dark cloud burst through the trees. It hovered in front of them. Zenda's whole body shook with fright.

"We've made it this far, Zenda," Camille said. "Don't give up now."

"But I hurt Sophia," Zenda said, "and the raft went out of control, and I ate the lura berries, and . . ."

The creature seemed to grow larger with every word.

"And we made it through the night,"

Camille said.

"And we found food to eat," Mykal added.

"And you used your *kani* to help me," Alexandra pointed out.

Zenda knew her friends were right. They had done all of those things. *She* had done all of those things. They were going to make it—but she had to take care of this thing—whatever it was—first.

She took a deep breath and faced the cloud. "I'm not afraid anymore. We'll make it back to the others. We'll get out of this."

Immediately, the dark cloud grew dimmer and the howling grew fainter.

"You tell it, Zenda!" Camille cried.

"I'm not afraid!" Zenda yelled. "I'm not! So you can just go back to where you came from!"

And the cloud vanished without a trace.

*One More Obstacle*

"Zenda, you did it!" Camille cried.

Zenda let out a deep breath. The only sound in the woods now was the peaceful chirping of birds.

And then the air in front of Zenda began to sparkle. A familiar sound, like tiny bells, filled the air.

Zenda held out her hand. A small crystal shard appeared in the air and gently floated into her palm.

"What's going on?" Alexandra asked as Camille and Mykal crowded around Zenda.

They watched as a red mist swirled around the piece of crystal. The mist formed letters that etched themselves onto the surface.

*When you face your fears, they no longer have power over you.*

"That looks like a musing," Alexandra said.

"It is," Zenda said, not taking her eyes off the crystal shard in her hand. "That's how I get them. They just kind of appear out of nowhere."

"That's pretty amazing," Alexandra said, and the tone in her voice sounded sincere, for once.

Camille hugged Zenda. "I can't believe you got another one!"

Zenda carefully dropped the small piece of her gazing ball into the pouch around her neck. Then she pulled the string until it was tightly closed.

"I don't know what makes me happier," she said. "Getting a musing, or getting rid of that weird thing from my dream."

"I'm happy about both," Mykal said, smiling at her.

Zenda knew Persuaja would be excited to see the new musing. Thinking of the psychic made Zenda remember what Persuaja had said about her nightmare: *Your dream is a part of you.* Persuaja had been right, of course. Zenda wondered if defeating the monster in the dream meant she would be a braver person from now on. She hoped so. They still had to find a way home.

"I'm sorry I left the trail," she said. "Are we going to be able to get back?"

"We didn't come far," Mykal replied. "And the way we went crashing through the woods, it should be easy to find our way back."

Mykal was right. Their dash through the woods had left a trail of flattened earth and broken shrubbery. They followed the trail back to the clearing, then down the hill to the riverbank.

Alexandra had several questions for Zenda as they walked back.

"How many musings do you have?" she asked.

Something in Alexandra's voice made Zenda feel comfortable answering. "Today was the sixth one," she said.

Alexandra nodded. "I have six too. They kind of appear floating inside the gazing ball."

Zenda nodded. "Camille told me."

They were silent for a while, and then Alexandra spoke again.

"I'm sorry about the way I acted yesterday," she said in a low voice. "I got scared when the raft got stuck in the rocks. It's just . . . I can't swim."

Zenda was surprised. She had never imagined that Alexandra could be scared of anything. She definitely knew how bad that could make you feel.

"It's okay," Zenda said, and she meant it.

Behind them, Mykal cried out.

"Hey, isn't that a waterfall up there?"

Zenda looked out onto the river. Sure enough, there was a small river up ahead, pouring down toward them. It had to be the same waterfall that carried them down the current.

"Then we're not far," Camille said. "Marion Rose said that it was a short hike back to the campsite from where the rafts landed."

Mykal brushed past the girls and broke into a run. Zenda, Camille, and Alexandra followed him.

Then Mykal stopped in his tracks. "Hold on," he said.

The trail in front of them descended into a deep gully. It must have been an offshoot of the river at one time, Zenda guessed, but now it was just a deep, dry pit about twelve feet wide—too far to jump across.

"We'll have to climb it," Zenda said.

"But look how steep the sides are," Mykal pointed out. "We can get down there, but I'm not so sure we can get back out."

Alexandra moaned. "We are going to be stuck on this stupid moon forever!"

Working
Together

"No we're not," Zenda said quickly. "We've come this far. We can do it."

"Sure we can," Camille added. "There are four of us. We can help one another."

Mykal looked thoughtful. "Maybe, if we had some vines to help us . . ."

Zenda looked back at the forest. "I'll get some."

Camille joined her, and they came back with a long strand of thick vine. Mykal took it from them and wrapped it around his shoulders.

"All right," he said. "Let's try it."

They cautiously began their descent down into the gully. Zenda found it easier to slide, slowing herself down with her feet.

Soon they were all at the bottom. From down there, the steep walls of the gully looked even higher and more difficult to climb. But Mykal had a plan.

"You three can give me a boost," he said. "Then when I get to the top, I'll throw down

120

the vine."

The girls put their hands together, forming a platform for Mykal to stand on. He stepped up, then strained his arms to reach the top of the gully. Once he gripped hold, they helped push his legs up.

"Made it!" he cried, looking down from the top. "I'll throw down the vine. You can use it to climb up."

"It's not going to be easy for whoever's last," Alexandra said, frowning.

The marks from the blue stingers still glowed a faint pink on Alexandra's arms. Alexandra had been through a lot today.

"You can go next," Zenda and Camille said at the same time.

Alexandra gave a grateful smile. "Thanks."

Zenda and Camille boosted Alexandra as high as they could. She grabbed onto the vine and used it to pull herself to the top of the gully.

Zenda turned to her friend. "You go

next," she said. "After getting rid of that thing from my dreams, I feel like I can do anything."

"I know you can," Camille said. Zenda helped push her up the side of the gully, and Camille grabbed the vine and pulled herself up the rest of the way.

Zenda looked up. Mykal, Camille, and Alexandra looked down at her. They had the vine safely anchored in their arms.

"Brace your feet against the side of the gully," Mykal instructed. "And use your arms to pull you up."

Zenda nodded and took a deep breath. She grabbed hold of the vine.

*Keep calm,* she told herself, remembering the crazy way the vines had reacted to her nervousness yesterday. *You can do this!*

Zenda pushed her feet against the gully wall and then began to pull herself up the vine. Her arms strained with the effort.

"You're doing it, Zen!" Camille called down.

*One, two. One, two.* Zenda slowly climbed up. Her arms felt like jelly now. She was sure she couldn't make it. She was going to slip, to fall back down into the gully . . .

"I can't hold on!" Zenda cried.

Immediately, three pairs of arms reached down, grabbed her, and pulled her up. Zenda gratefully collapsed on the ground.

"Thanks," she breathed.

"No problem," Mykal said. "It's a lot easier when we all help one another, isn't it?"

No one could argue with that. They dusted themselves off and began marching back up the river.

They hadn't gone far when they saw the clearing where the other rafts had landed the day before. But the clearing wasn't empty. A tent had been posted in the center, and Zenda saw four figures around it.

"Hey, I see them!" a voice cried out.

The figures came running toward them. Red-haired Ferris came first, followed by

Torin, Darius, and Wei Lan.

Mykal charged off toward them, practically knocking Ferris down. The two boys slapped palms.

"What happened to you?" Ferris asked. "It looks like you've been wrestling bears or something."

Zenda realized they must look pretty scraggly. Their clothes were stained with dirt, and were still slightly damp from the day before. Zenda and Alexandra had lost their flower crowns on the raft ride, and Camille's yellow flowers had shriveled up long ago.

"Perhaps our missing travelers would like some food and rest before they tell their story, Ferris," Wei Lan said. "Is everyone all right?"

Zenda, Mykal, Alexandra, and Camille looked at one another. Then they broke out into huge grins.

"We're fine," Zenda said. "Just fine."

Wei Lan led them back to the tent and

fed them peanut butter and dried apple slices from the supply of provisions the teachers had brought. He explained that a search party of Aquarian rangers had been out looking for them since yesterday, but hadn't found them. Wei Lan and the boys had decided to camp at the rafting spot in case they showed up.

"Good decision," Mykal said, stuffing an apple slice smothered in peanut butter into his mouth.

"When you're feeling up to it, we'll head back to the campsite," Wei Lan said. "We're all due back at the transport center in just a few hours."

Zenda didn't want to leave the comfort of the tent, but the hike back to the campsite ended up being fun. Ferris, Torin, and Darius listened, wide-eyed, to their story.

"You really got stung by blue stingers?" Torin asked Alexandra.

She proudly held out her arm. "Got the stings to prove it."

When they got back to camp, everyone surrounded them, cheering.

"Wait till you hear what happened to them!" Ferris announced, and they found themselves telling the story all over again. Zenda blushed furiously when Mykal told everyone about defeating the creature from her dreams. Several girls crowded around, asking to see the piece of her gazing ball.

Marion Rose broke through the crowd. "Back to work, everyone! We've got to get camp packed up and head back to the transport station in thirty minutes. Hop to it!"

The crowd dispersed, and Marion Rose walked up to Zenda and gave her a hug.

"That was an amazing story," she said. "I'm proud of you for getting over your fears."

"Thanks," Zenda said. "I'm proud of all of us for surviving. I never thought I could do it. And I did!"

Marion Rose smiled. "So are you glad you came on this trip?"

Zenda nodded. "I am. I think I'd do it again!"

The air sparkled again, and another glass shard appeared, accompanied by the sound of bells. Zenda gasped. A second musing, so soon? She caught it in her hand and watched the words form.

*A chance not taken is an opportunity missed.*

"Wow, Zenda," Marion Rose said. "You are on a roll today!"

*Enough!*

Word got around that Zenda had received another musing, and more girls gathered around to take a look at it. It was an odd feeling. Zenda was used to getting attention for doing embarrassing things, not good things.

Zenda walked with Camille and Sophia back on the trail to the transport center. Sophia's ankle was just fine, to Zenda's relief.

Zenda was telling Sophia how she got some of her other musings when Alexandra's voice rose up behind them.

"I *told* Marion Rose that Zenda's *kani* was dangerous," Alexandra was saying. "But she didn't listen. And then Zenda went ahead and ate those lura berries, even though I told her not to. That creepy monster she conjured up could have killed us all!"

Zenda froze in her tracks. Alexandra was talking to Gena, Astrid, and a few other girls in class. They clucked sympathetically at Alexandra's story. Then they all turned and glared at Zenda.

"That girl is a menace," Gena agreed. "You should tell your mother."

"Oh, I'm going to," Alexandra said. She was the only one in the group who didn't look at Zenda.

"I can't believe it," Zenda muttered. "She was being so nice just a little while ago. She apologized and everything."

Camille shook her head sympathetically. "You know what they say. A tigris butterfly never changes its stripes."

"I've never heard that before," Sophia said. "But if it means that Alexandra will always act mean, no matter what, then you're right."

"Well, I'm sick of it," Zenda said. She marched back toward Alexandra.

"I don't know what your problem is," Zenda told her. "You can lie all you want to. I don't care. As far as I'm concerned, you don't exist anymore."

A brief look of shock crossed Alexandra's face. Then she broke out into that crocodile smile of hers. "Of course you're upset," she said. "I'd be upset too, if I put the lives of three innocent people in danger. That must be hard for you."

"Did somebody just say something?" Zenda replied. "Because I didn't hear anything."

She turned around and stomped back toward Sophia and Camille.

"Serves her right," Sophia said.

Camille sighed. "I guess things will never get better between you two."

"No," Zenda said, and the thought made her surprisingly sad. "I guess they won't."

The transport to Azureblue went smoothly, and Zenda found herself immediately surrounded by her parents, who welcomed her with hugs.

"We heard you got lost," Verbena said. "My poor baby!"

"Mom!" Zenda protested. Verbena was

squeezing her so tight, she couldn't breathe. But she didn't exactly mind it, either.

Back home, the first thing Zenda did was put the pieces of her gazing ball in the box with the others. After a long bath, Vetiver stuffed her with sesame noodles topped with ginger, mushrooms, and shredded carrots, followed by peach sorbet and fresh strawberries. Zenda slipped on her pajamas and sank into her comfortable bed. Oscar hopped on her lap. She gave Luna a welcome-home squeeze, then picked up her journal and began to write.

———⊶⊷———

I learned a lot on Aquaria. Like that I can do things I never thought I could. And that facing my fears is easier than running from them.

That's why I'm not going to let Alexandra get to me anymore. I'm tired of it. If she doesn't leave me alone, I'm going to show her that I can be just as mean as she is.

We start school again in two days. At supper, Verbena told me that a new family moved into the village. There's a girl my age who'll be starting school with us. I wonder what she's like? I hope she's nicer than Alexandra.

What am I saying? <u>Everyone</u> is nicer than Alexandra.

I'm glad I still have two days off, because I want to go see Persuaja. I miss her. And I can't wait to tell her about my two new musings!

Two more musings! Can you believe it? That makes seven now. I've only got six more to get. That means I'm more than halfway there! Maybe I'll get all of my musings before my thirteenth birthday, after all. For the first time, I feel like I can do it.

And why not? If I survived being lost on Aquaria, I can do anything!

Cosmically yours,
Zenda